CAPER!

by
MONA MILLER

illustrated by DARIO BRIZUELA
and SIMONE BUONFANTINO

A GOLDEN BOOK • NEW YORK

RHUS39301

 Published in the United States by Golden Books, an imprint of Random House Children's Books, a division of Penguin Random House LLC, 1745 Broadway, New York, NY 10019, and in Canada by Penguin Random House Canada Limited, Toronto.
Golden Books, A Golden Book, and the G colophon are registered trademarks of Penguin Random House LLC.

rhcbooks.com
dcsuperherogirls.com
dckids.com

ISBN 978-1-5247-6603-0

PENCIL MANUFACTURED IN CHINA

Book Printed in the United States of America

10 9 8 7 6 5 4 3 2 1

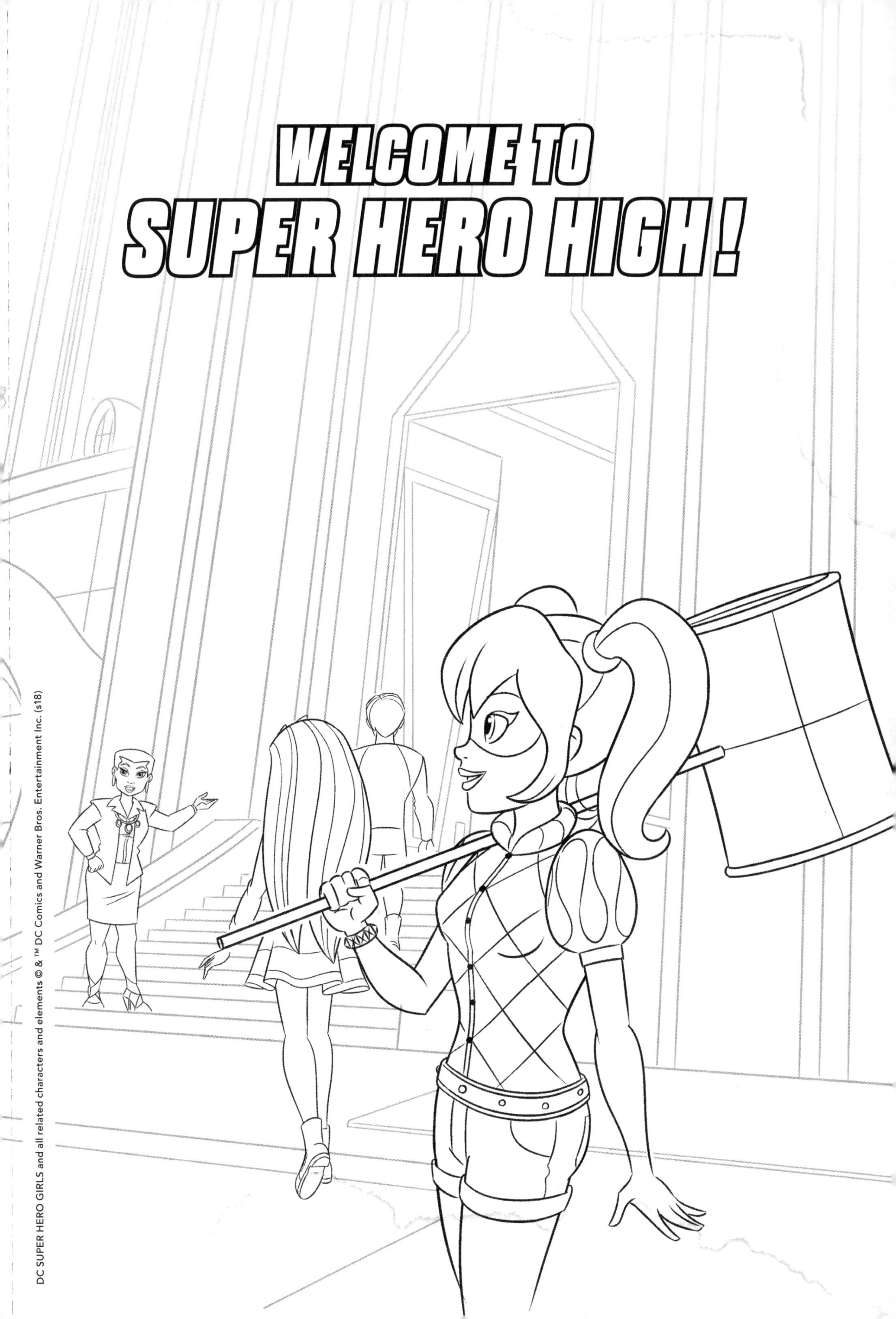
WELCOME TO
SUPER HERO HIGH!

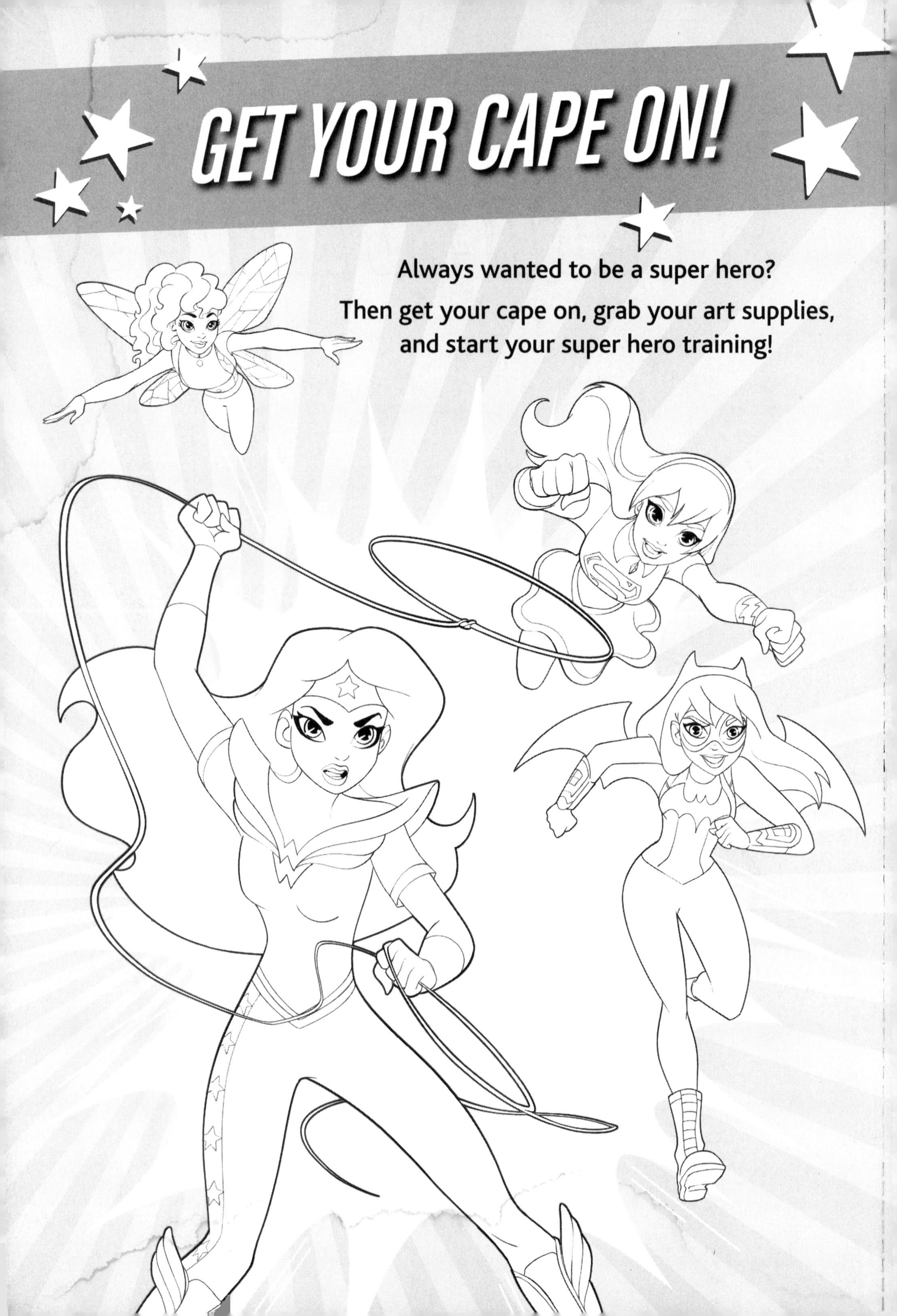
GET YOUR CAPE ON!
Always wanted to be a super hero?
Then get your cape on, grab your art supplies,
and start your super hero training!

Wonder Woman is an Amazon.
Complete her shield and draw
her Golden Lasso of Truth.

Supergirl is about to go head-to-head
with a big bad robot.
Color the scene.

Batgirl is on patrol over the city of Metropolis.
Draw her Batrope and what she is swinging from.

Katana is practicing with a classmate.
Who is she working out with?
Draw the scene.

Poison Ivy's plants are
growing wildly around her.
Draw them.

Draw Hawkgirl in an action scene.

https://www.

Harley Quinn just got some great footage for Harley's Quinntessentials. Draw a funny scene at Super Hero High.

Wonder Woman welcomes you to Super Hero High.
Draw yourself as a super hero alongside her.

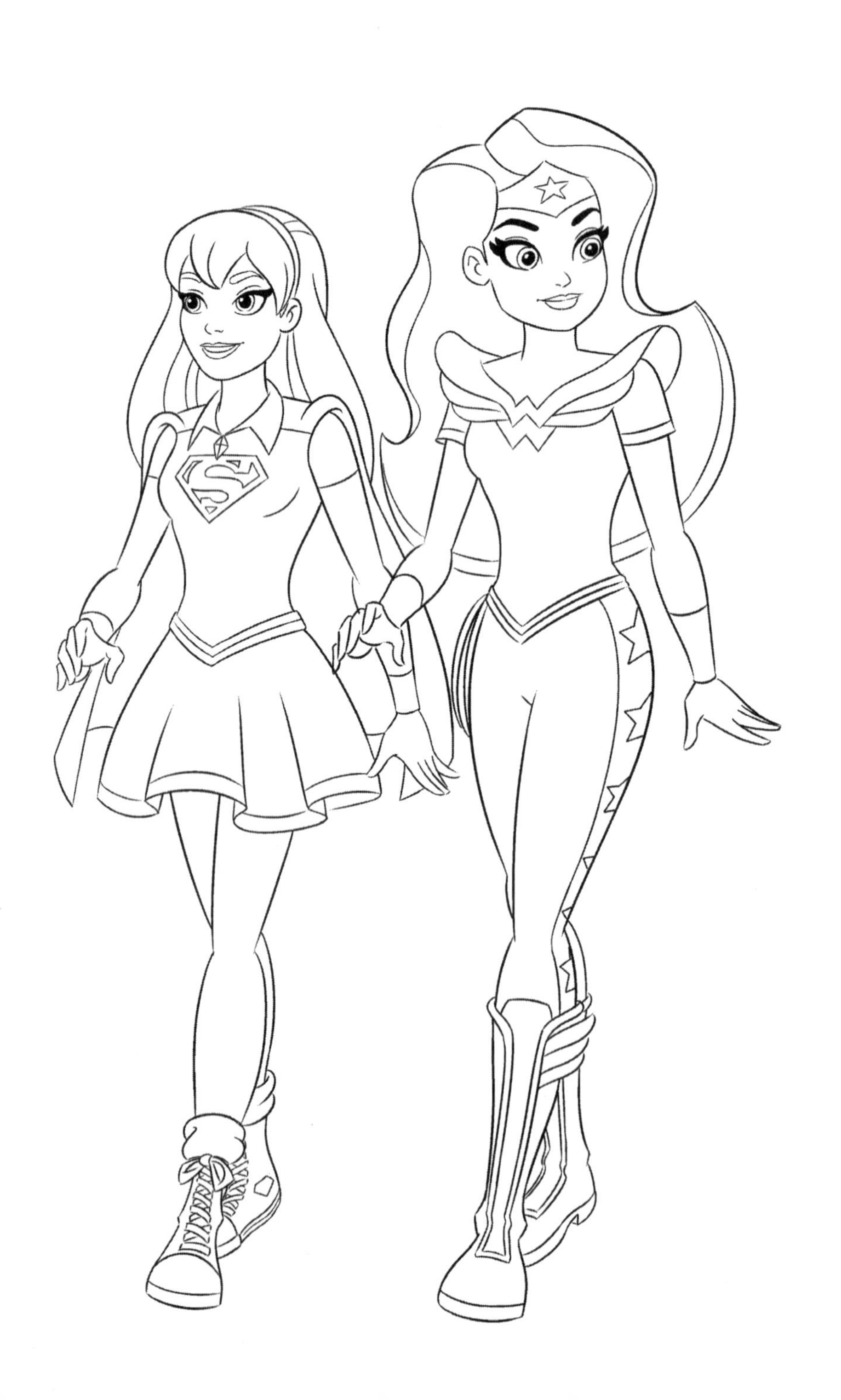

ABOUT ME

NAME: ....

AGE: ....

INTERESTS: ....

....

....

....

WHY I WANT TO BE A SUPER HERO: ....

....

....

....

....

....

MY SUPER HERO NAME

Choose one word from each column below to help you find your super hero name, or just make up your own name from scratch!

Ultra	Girl
Brain	Woman
Mega	Fire
Shadow	Cat
Lightning	Teen
Poison	Bee
Atomic	Star
Power	Ivy
Beast	Claw
Iron	Hawk

?

Write your super hero name in the space below.

MY SUPER HERO SYMBOL

Wonder Woman has an awesome symbol!

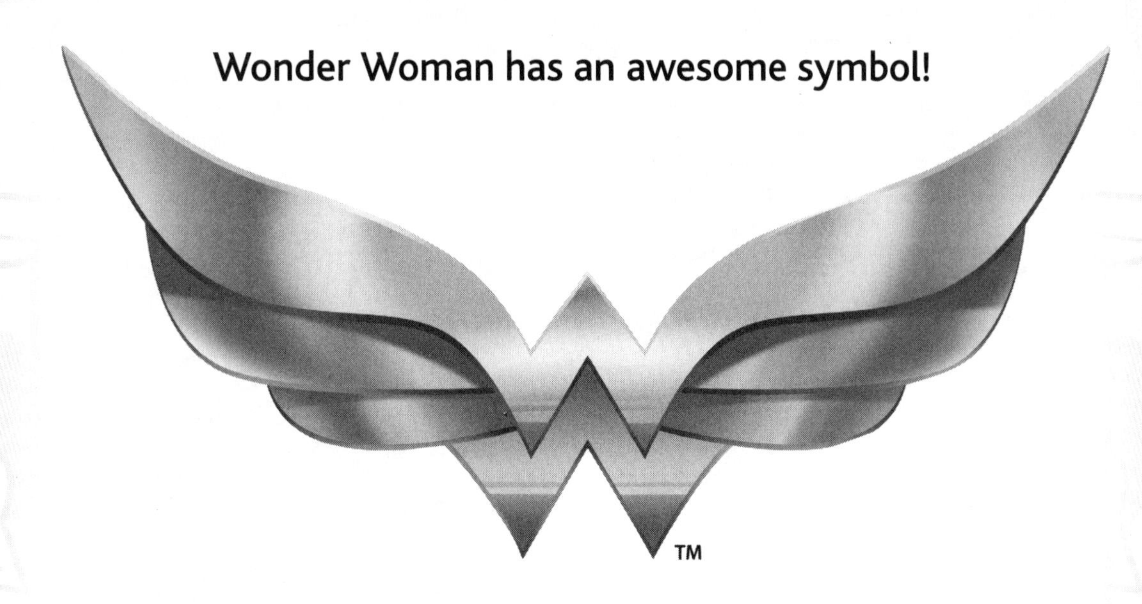

Create your own symbol for your super hero identity here.

MY SUPER HERO STYLE

Design and label
your own super hero
outfit and accessories.
Make sure your
costume is practical
for racing around and
fighting crime in!

Imagine yourself as a student at Super Hero High.
Design your cape.

SUPER SUIT DESIGN CLASS

Crazy Quilt has an assignment for you.
Draw your own version of Supergirl's costume,
or design a totally new one!

Decorate Supergirl's cape.

SUPER SUIT DESIGN CLASS

Crazy Quilt has an assignment for you.
Draw your own version of Batgirl's costume,
or design a totally new one!

SUPER SUIT DESIGN CLASS

Crazy Quilt has an assignment for you. Draw your own version of Bumblebee's costume, or design a totally new one!

Extra credit: Draw Bumblebee as small as you can.

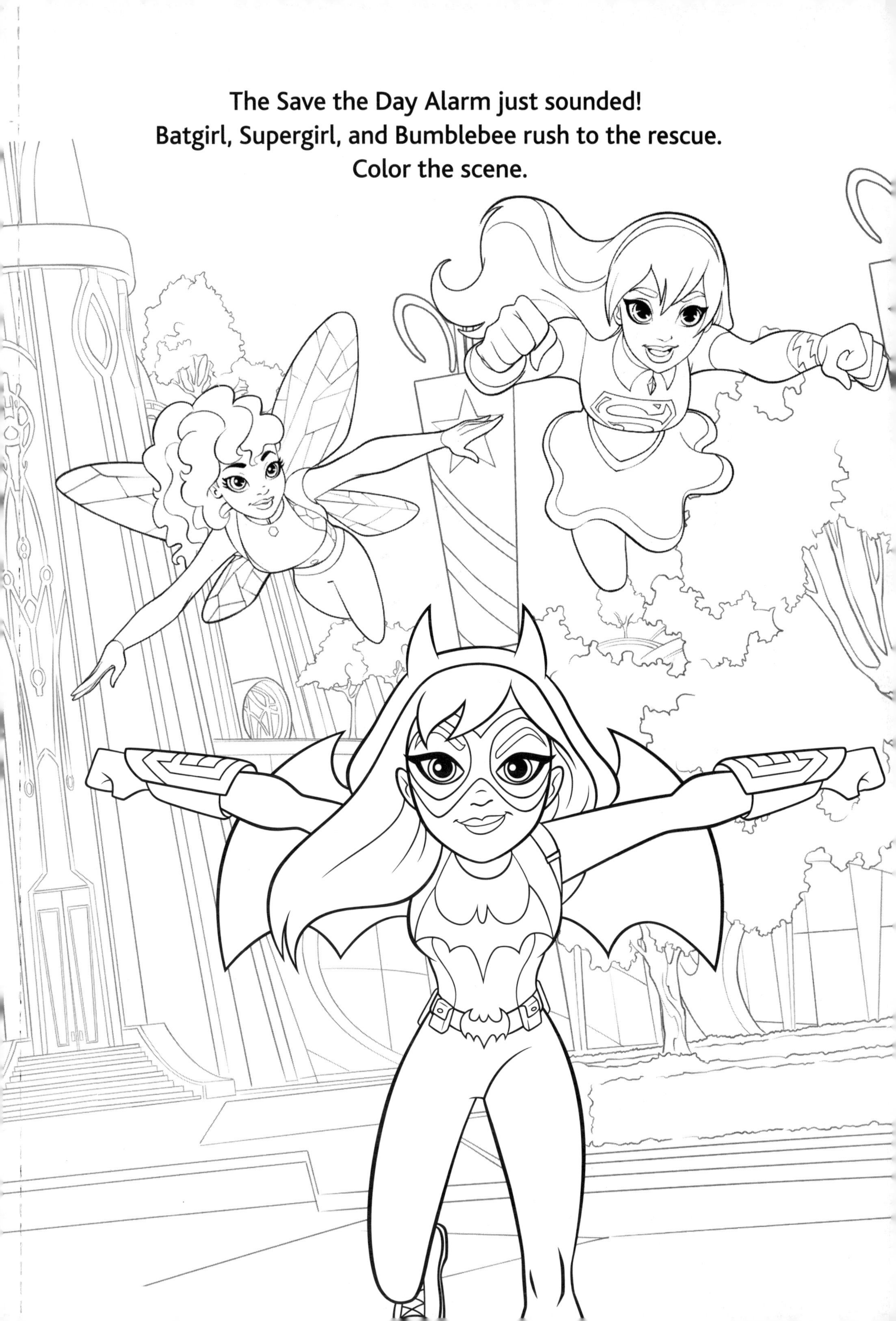
The Save the Day Alarm just sounded!
Batgirl, Supergirl, and Bumblebee rush to the rescue.
Color the scene.

Wonder Woman has lassoed
a villain who's up to no good.
Draw the bad guy.

SUPER SUIT DESIGN CLASS

Crazy Quilt has an assignment for you.
Draw your own version of Wonder Woman's costume,
or design a totally new one!

Bumblebee is a member of the Junior Detective Society,
and she just found a clue. Color the scene.

MISSING
DO NOT EAT!

LUNCH TIME!

Help The Flash find the path to his favorite food.

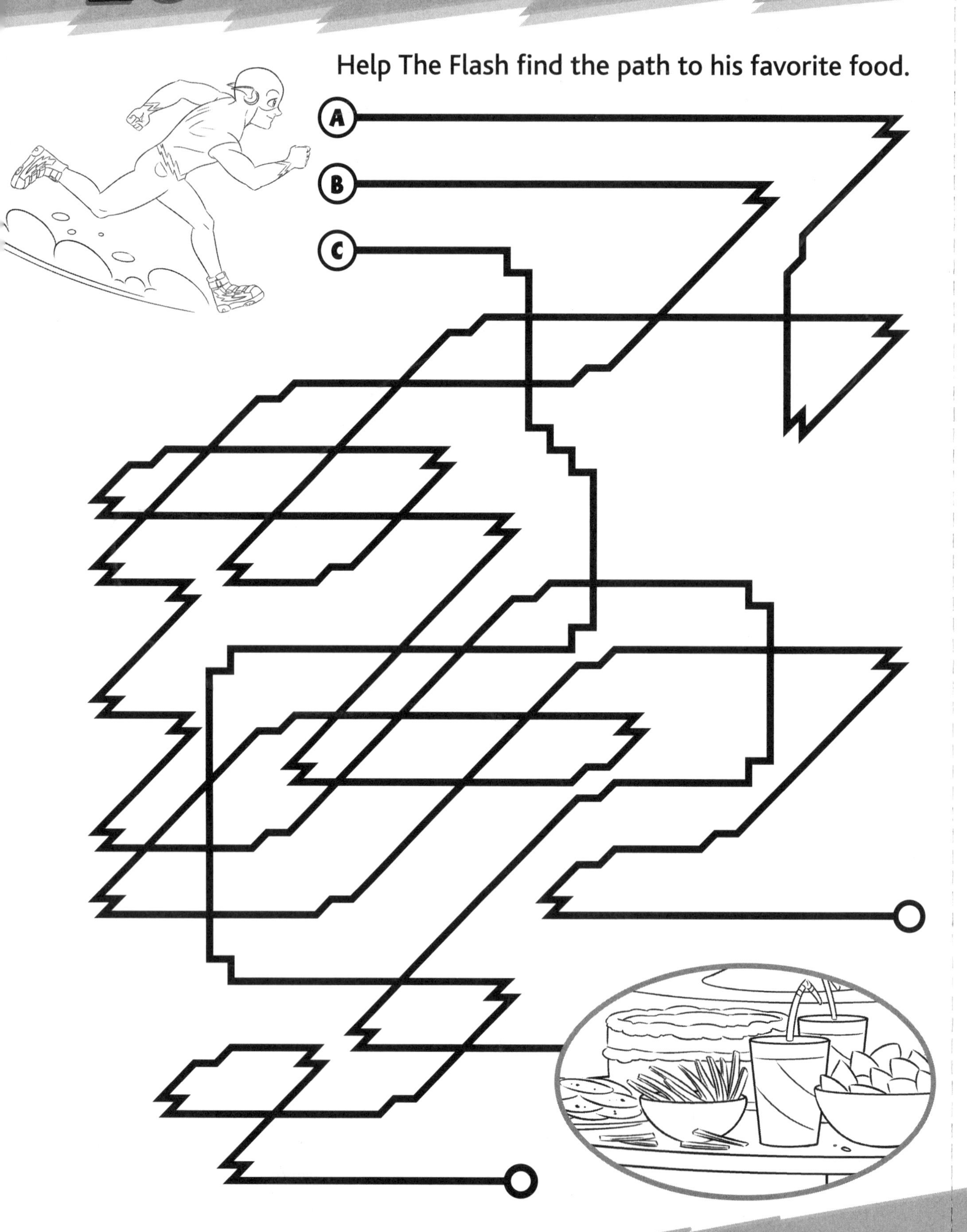

Answer: B

Cheetah challenges The Flash
to a race. Draw the scene below.
Who is the winner?

Supergirl is racing Hawkgirl. Who do you think will win?

SUPER SUIT DESIGN CLASS

Crazy Quilt has an assignment for you.
Draw your own version of Hawkgirl's costume,
or design a totally new one!

Draw Miss Martian
sneaking up on Harley Quinn.

SUPER SUIT DESIGN CLASS

Crazy Quilt has an assignment for you.
He thinks Miss Martian needs a bold, fresh look.
Design a totally new and dynamic costume for her!

Katana is a master with the sword.

Help her create a new costume masterpiece.

SUPER SUIT DESIGN CLASS

Crazy Quilt has an assignment for you. Draw your own version of Katana's costume, or design a totally new one!

Lady Shiva sometimes uses her hair like a whip.
Draw her long braided hair in action,
or give her a fun new hairstyle!

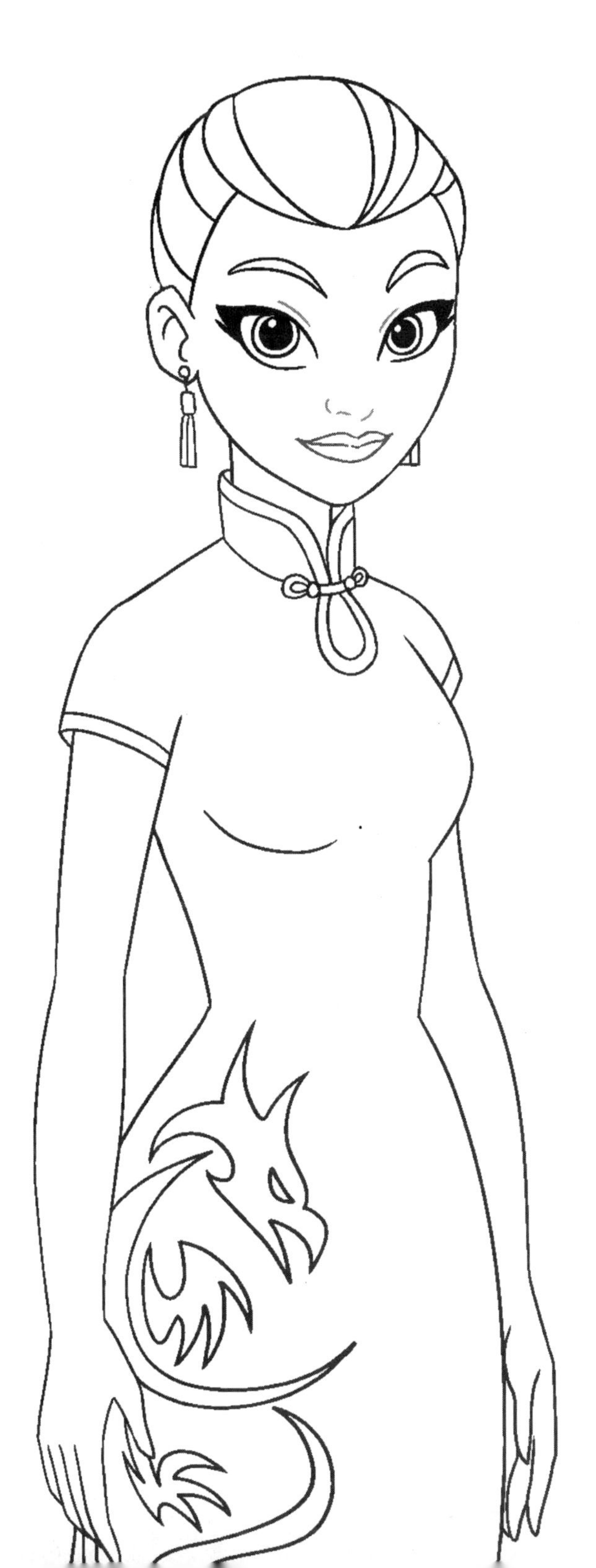

Sister team Thunder and Lightning pack a lot of power.
Draw them crackling with energy.

SHOCK AND AWESOME

Thunder can create powerful shock waves.
Draw her delivering a devastating blast.

SUPER SUIT DESIGN CLASS

Crazy Quilt has an assignment for you. It's not her style, but Big Barda needs a formal dress for an intergalactic party.

Big Barda rushed into battle and forgot a few things.
Draw her helmet, cape, and
most importantly, her Mega Rod.

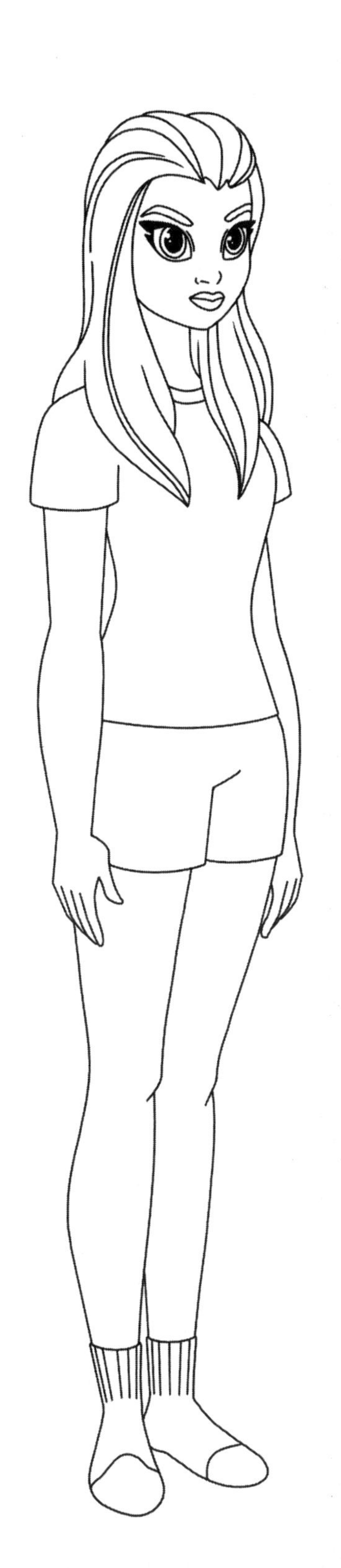

Draw yourself doing a
fabulous handstand just like Harley!

SUPER SUIT DESIGN CLASS

Crazy Quilt has an assignment for you.
Draw your own version of class clown Harley Quinn's costume, or design a totally new one!

Art teacher, June Moon, wants you to create a masterpiece. Draw it here.

Starfire is an alien who can fly
and fire powerful starbolts.
Draw her in an outer-space scene.

Hawkgirl loves to spread
her wings and soar.
Draw her outstretched wings.

When Lightning's costume came back from the cleaners, the electrical bolts were gone. Add the missing details to her costume.

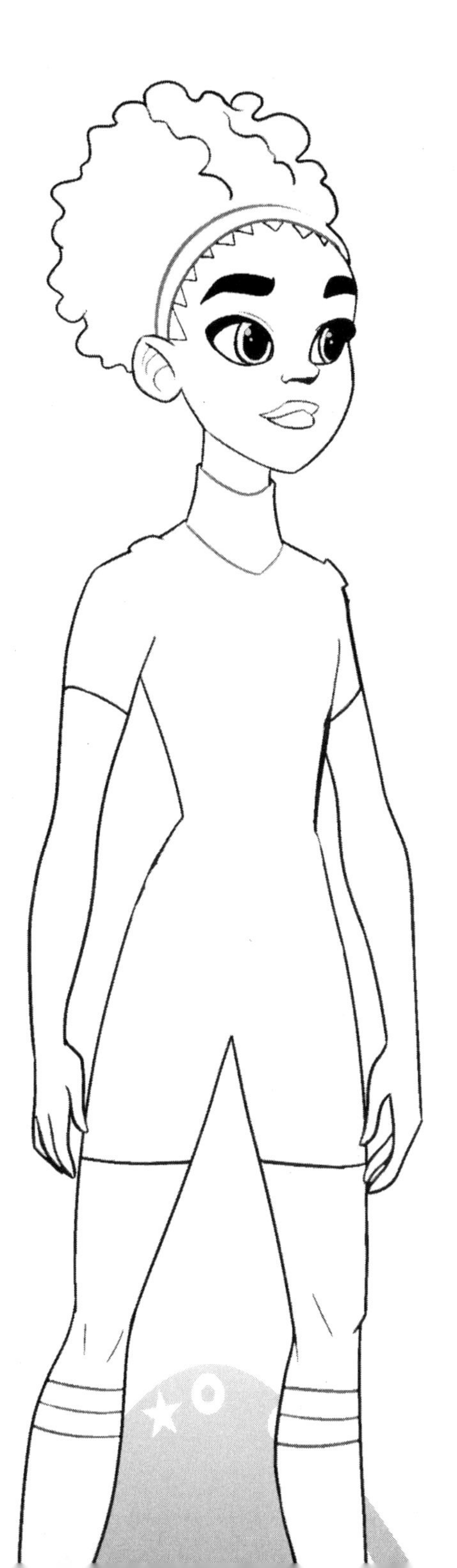

Star Sapphire flies through outer space.
Draw the scene and don't forget her power ring!

RING OF POWER

Green Lantern and Star Sapphire have different symbols on their power rings. Imagine what kind of power ring you would have. Design your own symbol.

The students at Super Hero High like to refuel and relax in the cafeteria. What's for lunch?

Complete the scene.

What's in Your Locker?

Draw it here.

Harley Quinn
just redecorated her room.
Color the wall as many colors as you like!

DORM ROOM DESIGNS

Design and decorate your room at Super Hero High School with your own super style.

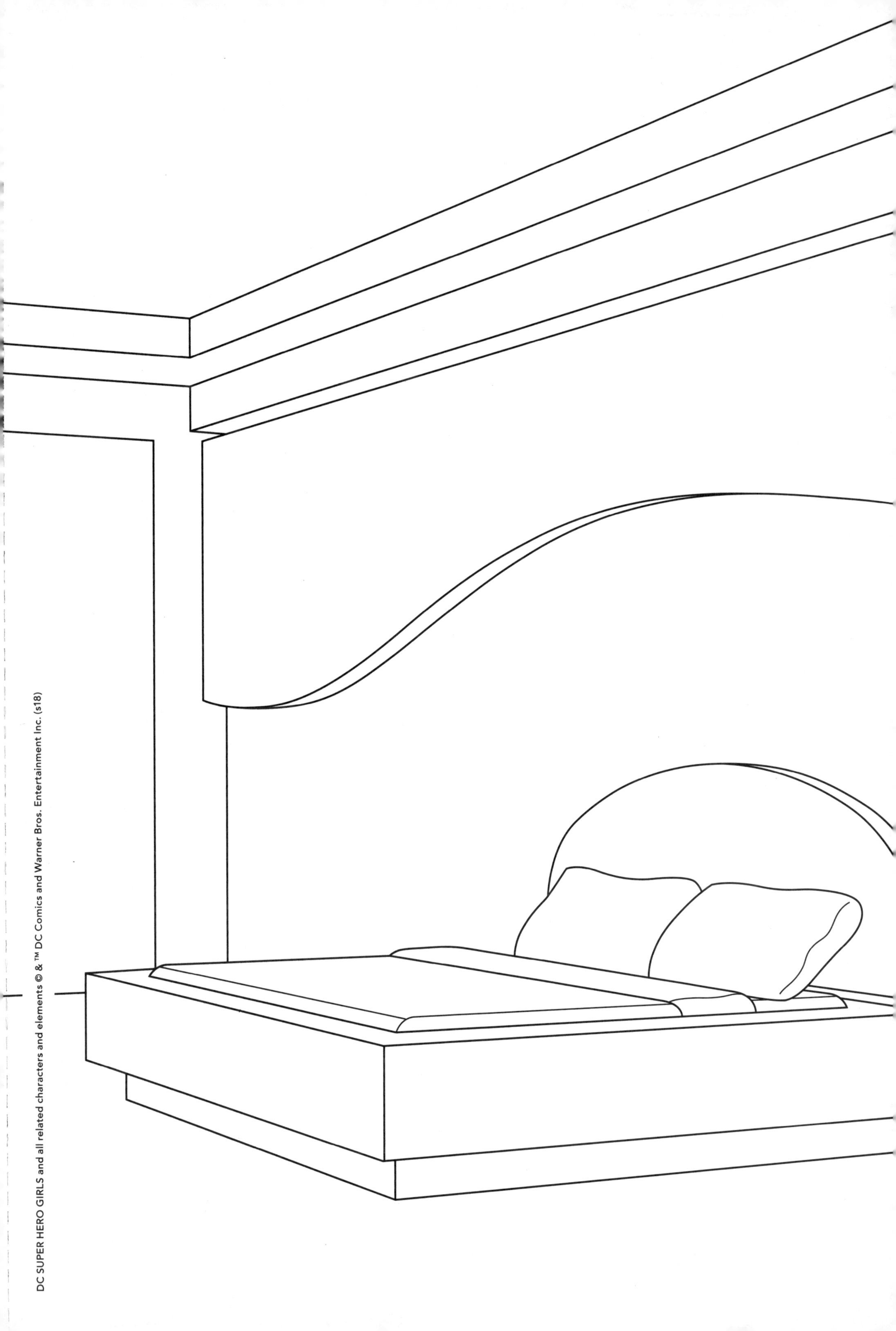

TRUE IDENTITY

Every super hero is unique. Doodle over these schoolbooks to show your truly individual super hero self.

SHHS

Super Hero Signatures

One day you might become famous for all your good deeds!
Practice your signature here for giving your autograph.

Use this page to write a diary entry
that says a lot about you.

Batgirl is on patrol with her trusty Utility Belt.
List three things she might have packed
for her adventures.

1. ______________________________

2. ______________________________

3. ______________________________

Batgirl snares a bad guy with her Net Gun.
Draw the villain.

Supergirl sees something
with her X-ray vision.
Draw it.

What do you see?

Draw Wonder Woman using her indestructible bracelets to deflect lasers and projectiles.

1. 

2. ______________________________

3. ______________________________

4. ______________________________

5. ______________________________

Supergirl and Bumblebee want you to fly into action with them. Draw yourself.

Batgirl has designed all kinds of tech to help her fight crime.
Draw some computers and gadgets for her.

Cyborg just gave himself a major tech upgrade.
Draw his new armor.

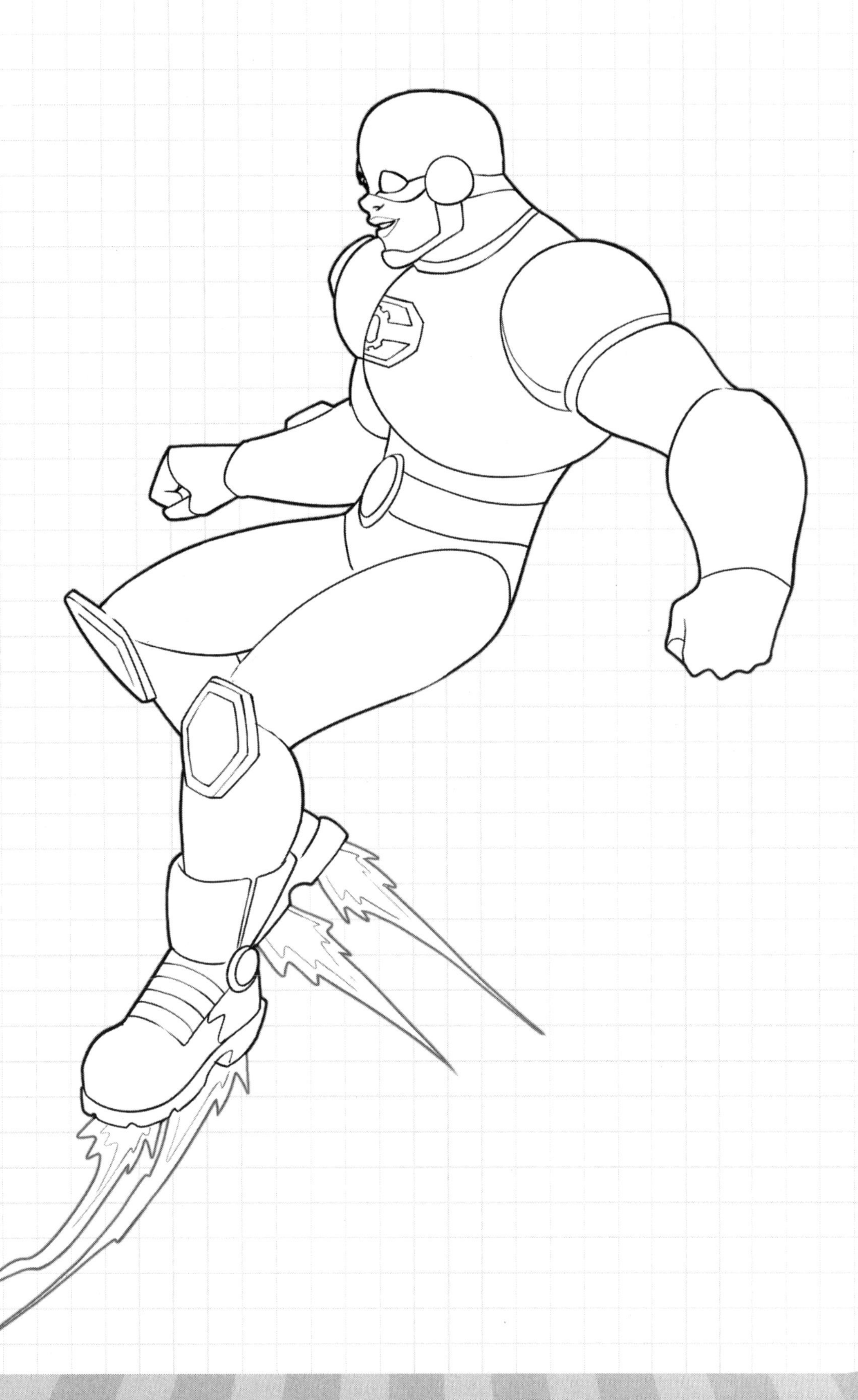

Everything is growing
in Poison Ivy's garden.
Color the scene.

Bad guys better keep clear of Catwoman. Draw her foe.

Catwoman is trapped underground!
Can you help her find her way to the surface?

WATCH OUT!

Draw what you think Wonder Woman is punching.

Supergirl is super-strong
and she can really fly.
Draw what she is lifting
in the air.

Supergirl is late for class, when she realizes she forgot her cape! Draw it before Vice Principal Grodd sees her.

Poison Ivy's plant, Chompy, has grown bigger than ever.
Add details to it, such as teeth, eyes, and thorns.

Katana is in a band.
Draw her bandmates
rocking out.

What is Bumblebee blasting?
Draw the scene.

Poison Ivy's latest science experiment
has grown out of control.
Color the scene.

Katana is a master of stealth.
Is she sneaking up on a bad guy
or into a surprise party?

Draw the scene.

Poison Ivy entangles a foe in one of her thick vines.
Draw the villain.

Cyborg is battling a big bad robot.
Complete the scene.

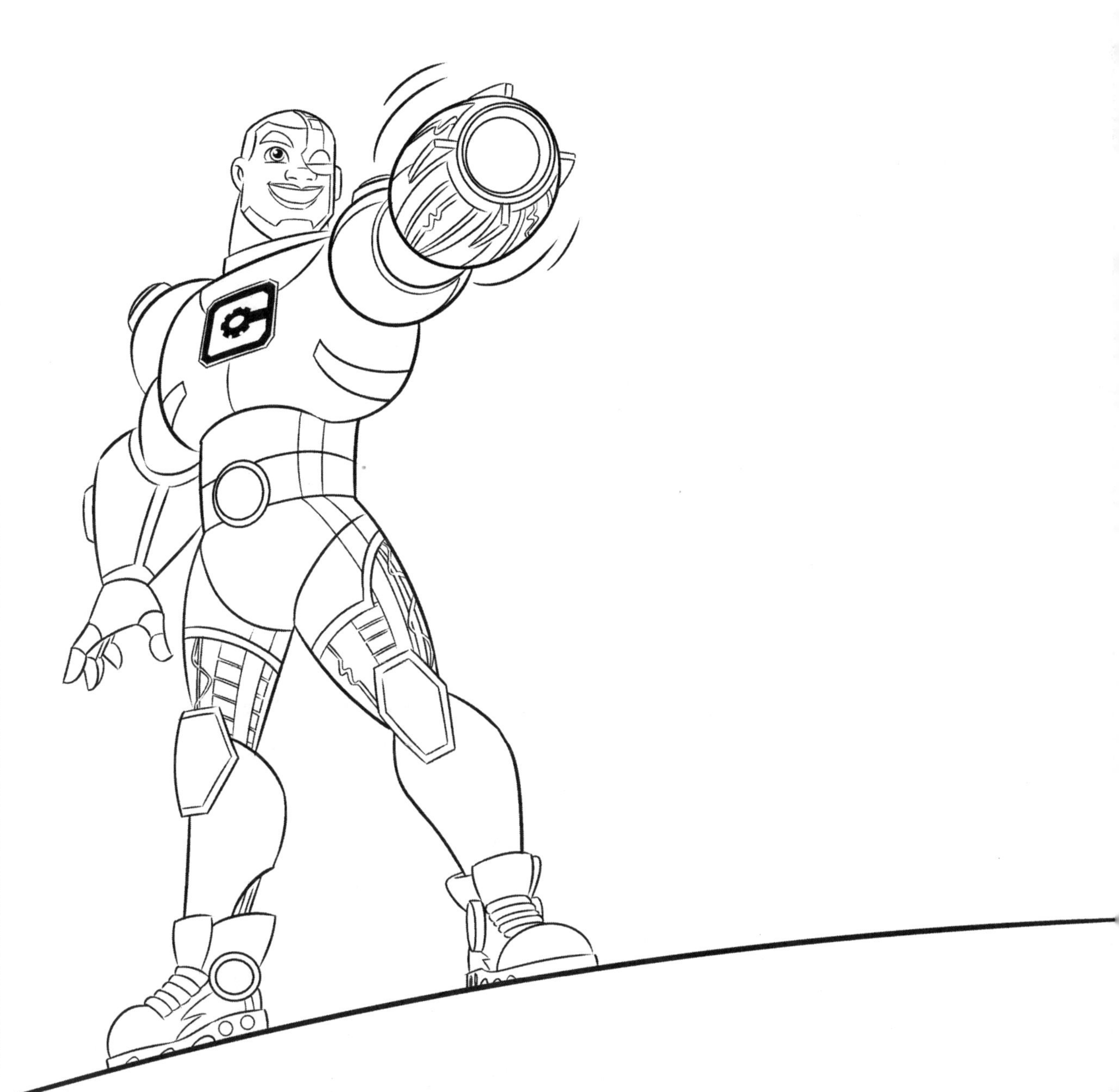

Star Sapphire can create anything she imagines with the violet energy in her power ring. Draw what you think she's making.

Harley Quinn is
bringing down her mallet.
Draw what she's smashing.

Imagine yourself as one of the Furies.
Design your mask or helmet.

START
FINISH
Go
head-to-head with
the golden-arrowed Fury
Artemiz to solve the
maze and see who's got
the best aim!

Cheetah is looking sharp!
Draw yourself next to her in the same outfit.

Frost is using her powers to create a spectacular ice sculpture. Help her make it extra cool!

MIGHTY MEALS

Steve Trevor is trying to come up with three new dishes to serve at Capes & Cowls Café. Think of a few ideas and write them here.

CAPES & COWLS CAFÉ

Appetizer

....

....

Main Course

....

....

Dessert

....

....

SUPER SNACK TIME

Beast Boy is hungry.
Draw another sandwich for him!

Beast Boy can transform into any animal.
What animal would you like to become?
Draw it here.

Pesky Parademons like Perry
can multiply and get out of control.
Draw your own Parademon below.

Krypto is a super pet.
What kind of super pet would you like to have?
Draw or describe it.

Catwoman is on the prowl.
Finish the scene.

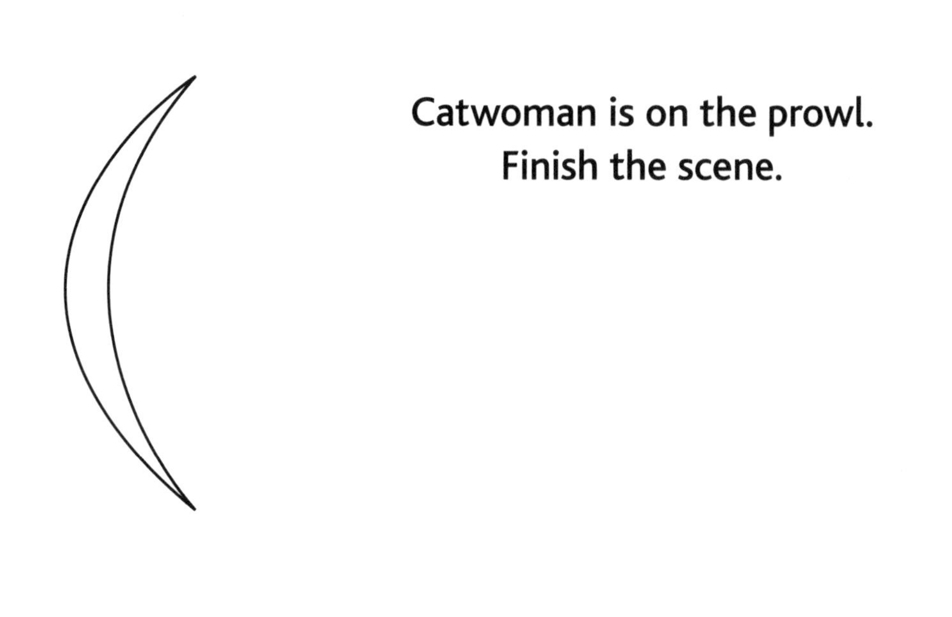

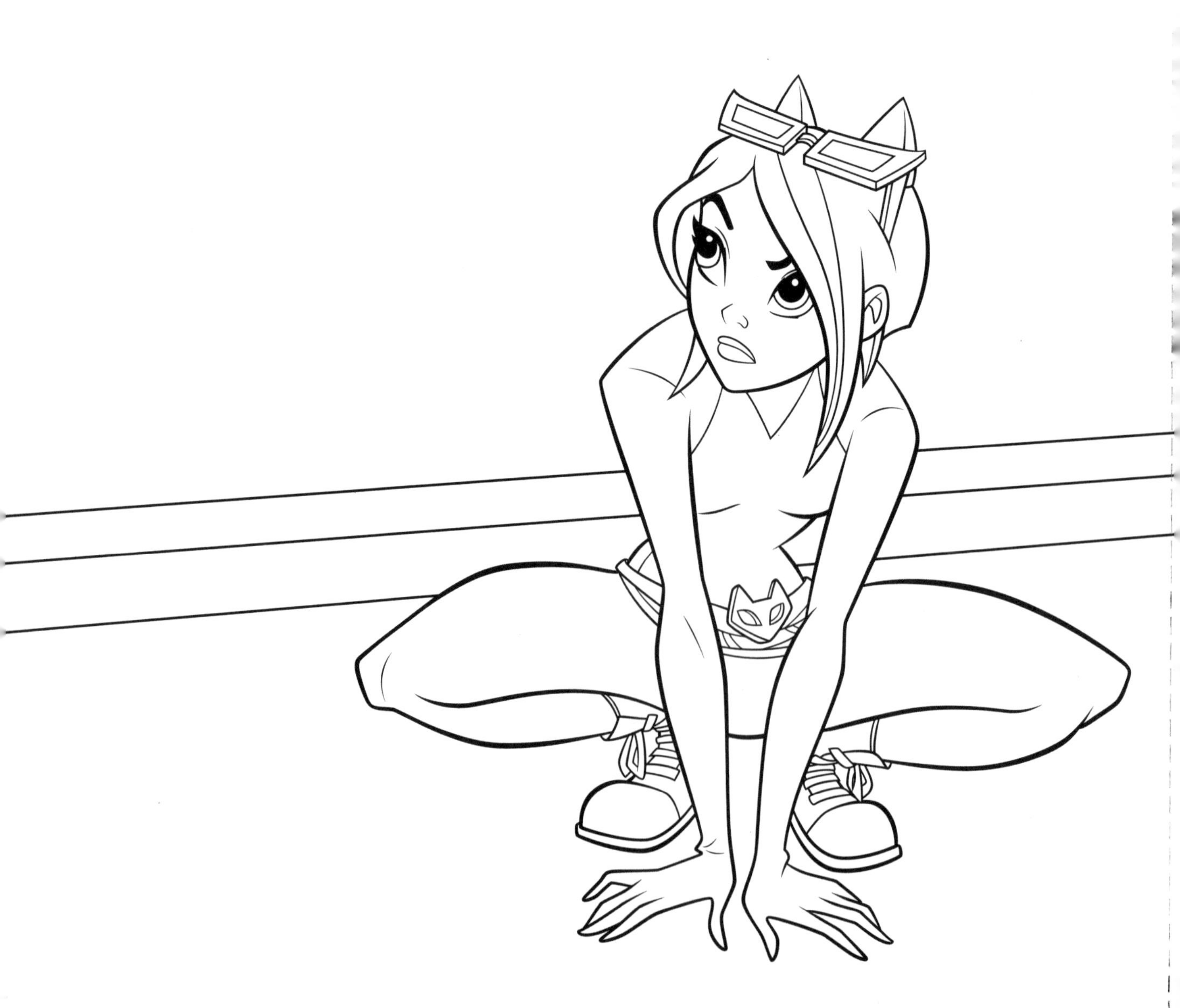

START
FINISH
Go head-to-head
with the fiendish Fury
Speed Queen to solve
the maze and see
who's faster!

SUPER HERO CODE

Make up your own code by drawing a different symbol or mark for each letter. Then use this code every time you need to pass on a top-secret message.

Practice writing a secret message in your code here.

What Makes You, You?

Write a list
of words that best
describe you.
Then use them
to draw a portrait
of yourself,
like these of
Harley Quinn and
Wonder Woman!

INVINCIBLE
COURAGEOUS
WONDER WOMAN
TOUGH
POW!
BRAVE
FLIGHT
STRONG
LEADER
TRUTH
JUSTICE
AMAZONIAN
PRINCESS
SUPERFAST
COMPETITIVE
AMAZING
OUTSTANDING

MAKE 'EM LAUGH!
Harley Quinn
loves telling jokes.
Come up with
a new one for
the fabulous
funny girl.

SUPERPOWER TOP 10

What are 10 things you would you do if you had superpowers?

1.

2.

3.

4.

5.

6.

7.

8.

9.

10.

MY SUPER HERO FRIENDS

Pack these pages with your favorite pictures of you and all your super hero friends. Remember to include captions explaining how you just saved the world!

Ace reporter Lois Lane has just cracked a case! Find the path to get her back to the *Daily Planet*.

Answer: B

Lois Lane is covering the story about how Metropolis was saved from a super-villain. Write a story to match the picture.

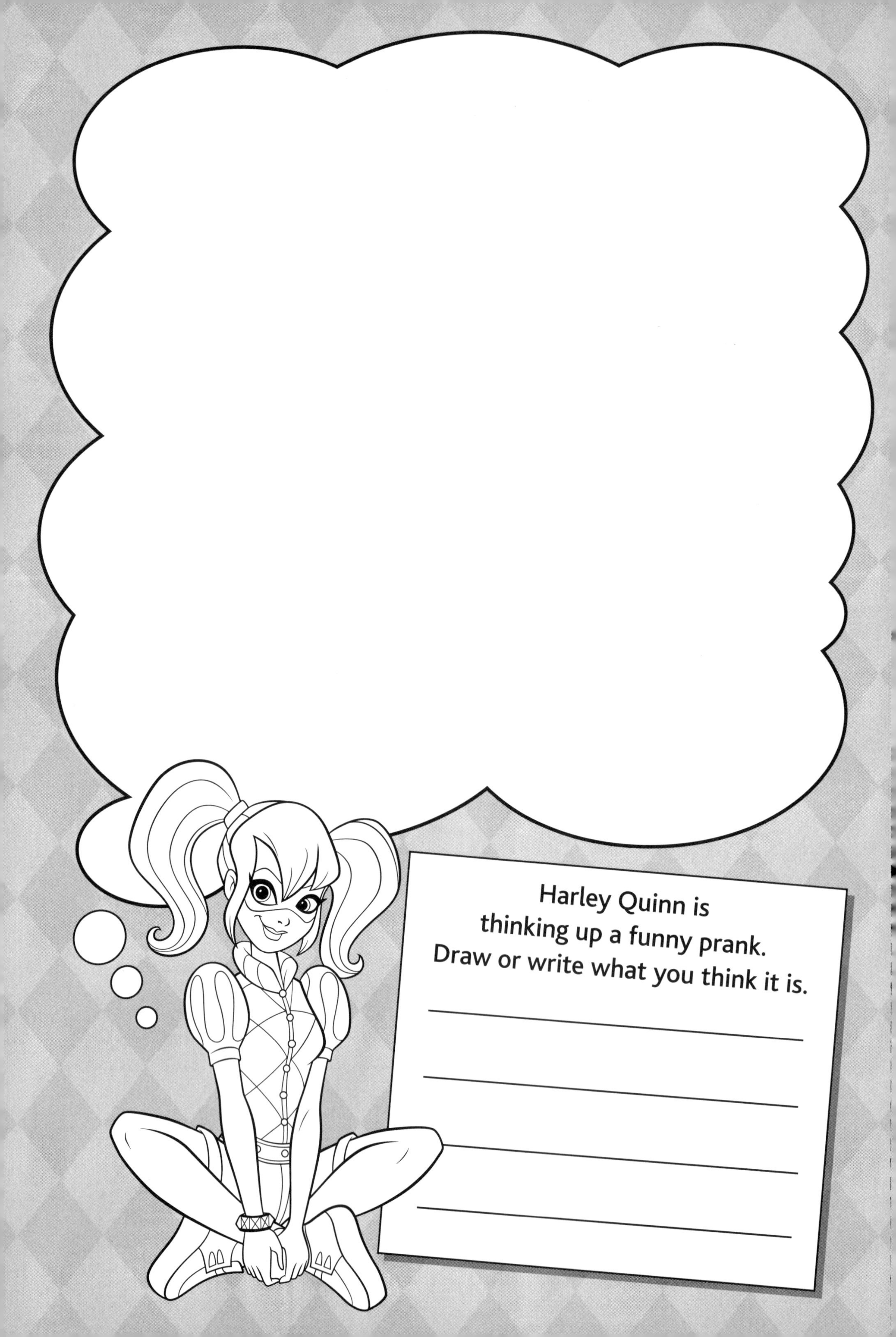
Harley Quinn is
thinking up a funny prank.
Draw or write what you think it is.

Harley Quinn is about to light a prank-cannon
in Weaponomics class.
Draw what will happen next.

Katana is about to defuse a glitter bomb
in Weaponomics class.

Wonder Woman is super-strong.
Draw what she is lifting.

Bumblebee just upgraded her wings.
Draw them.

NAME A FRIEND . . .

HERO OF THE MONTH!

And list five reasons why.

Name: ____________________

1. ____________________
2. ____________________
3. ____________________
4. ____________________
5. ____________________

WHAT WOULD WONDER WOMAN DO?

Imagine you're Wonder Woman for a day.
What would you do if you had
her skills and powers?
Fill these pages with your adventures.

Draw your favorite hero
smashing through a wall!

WANTED

Draw your favorite villain—or create a new one!

King Shark is causing trouble
under the sea.

Draw yourself saving the day with Wonder Woman and your favorite heroes.

Harley Quinn is in action.
Draw what's going on around her.

Color Harley's buggy.

Wonder Woman is racing Batgirl in her Invisible Jet.
Draw your own vehicle in the race.
Who will win?

Get your cape on and color the scene!

UNLEASH YOUR POWERS!

Choose superpowers, super gadgets, or amazing abilities to deal with each situation on the next page. Take inspiration from the DC Super Hero Girls' powers and gadgets!

THE DC SUPER HERO GIRLS' POWERS AND GADGETS:

Wonder Woman:
flight, Lasso of Truth, extra-powerful shield, bullet-deflecting bracelets

Bumblebee:
shrinking powers, tech genius, suit of strength, sonic sting blasts

Supergirl:
super-strength, heat vision, positivity

Harley Quinn:
acrobatics, quick wit

Katana:
samurai sword skills, martial-arts expertise, fearlessness

Batgirl:
computer genius, martial-arts expertise, advanced detective skills, Utility Belt

SITUATIONS

1. You're in an extremely tight situation—four heavy stone walls are closing in around you, and there's only a tiny space above to escape through! What do you do?

2. A sneaky cheat has been taking everyone's super hero homework books and copying from them. What do you do?

3. A mystery super-villain has hacked into Super Hero High School's computer system. What do you do?

4. Metropolis has been brought to a standstill by a terrible ice storm. Everything is frozen! What do you do?

WHICH DC SUPER HERO GIRL IS MOST LIKE YOU?

THE HERO OF THE MONTH IS . . .

Super Hero High is pleased to announce that the Hero of the Month is . . . YOU! Fill in your details below for this impressive award. You're the super hero who has shown helpfulness and selflessness and acted as an outstanding role model. You're awesome!

CONGRATULATIONS!

You saved the day, got an A+, and showed super hero skills along the way!

____

(your name here)

has successfully completed the first year of super hero training!